# HOW TO HAVE SEX FOR THE FIRST TIME

## Preventive measures for first sex

By

Dr Mirabella smith

# Table of contents

# Introduction

When most of us think of writing about sex, our minds turn to classic authors of explicit fornication (The Marquis de Sade, Anais Nin, Henry Miller, Erica Jong) or to contemporary erotic bestsellers (Fifty Shades of Grey, The Sexual Life of Catherine M., Wetlands). But often the best writing about sex can be found in books that are not about sex at all. Rather, many great novels portray sexual encounters as an inseparable part of the extraordinary ordinariness of daily life. What follows is a collection of credible, affecting sex scenes by writers who are celebrated not for their illicit content, but for their uncommonly precise prose and insightful observations of human nature. Rather than inviting you to gape at purely physical contortions, these scenes make the reader feel the acts described as bodily, emotional experiences that inform each character's unique sense of what it means to be alive.In The Good Mother by Sue Miller, a recently divorced woman meets a man who awakens her sexual longing for the first time. This would seem to be a familiar storyline: frigid female set free by confident, sexy hunk. But the form Anna's new passion takes is far from cliché or fantastic. Rather than swooning or feeling helpless and breathless in Leo's presence, Anna feels that her "pelvic bones got heavier, shifted somehow." And the first time they have sex, Anna does not experience multi-orgasmic fireworks, but a more realistic longing for the sex to last longer, to "feel more." With her ex-husband Brian and her prior lovers—starting with groping adolescent boys—Anna has always been passive, accepting male advances as "intrusions" to be endured, wanting the man to finish so the sex would end. But with Leo, Anna feels "left behind" when Leo comes, longing to experience the same pleasure he does. This is a far more interesting—and believable—depiction of the awakening of heterosexual female lust than, say, having your first orgasm when a man plays with your nipples (as happens to Anastasia in Fifty Shades of Grey).

For Anna, having pleasurable sex is not the magical result of good chemistry, but the logical result of wanting her own pleasure and eventually communicating her desires to her partner.

As you mature, you may start thinking about having sex for the first time. In addition to this, you may be wondering how it feels, how to handle any anxiety that may accompany it, and how to be safe.

*Chapter 1*

# what happens the first time you have sex?

Everyone's "first time" is different. But one of the most important parts of being prepared for sex is making sure you use birth control and condoms to help prevent pregnancy and STDs. Here's what happens when you lose your virginity.

Does it hurt to lose your virginity?

The first time you have vaginal sex, it may hurt, or feel good, or both. There might be pain and bleeding the first time a penis or fingers go into your vagina, but it doesn't happen to everybody. Some people naturally have more hymenal tissue than others — this pain and bleeding can happen when their hymen gets stretched.

If pain and bleeding doesn't get better after the first time you have vaginal sex (penis-in-vagina), you can slowly stretch your hymen tissue with your fingers over time to make it less painful. In rare cases, people may need to see a doctor for a small procedure to open their hymen. If you're worried about your hymen or have pain during sex, talk with your doctor or visit your local Planned Parenthood health center.

You may also have pain or irritation during vaginal sex if your vagina isn't lubricated (wet) enough. It's totally normal to not have a lot of vaginal lubrication, and it doesn't mean anything is wrong with you or your partner. Using lube can help make sex more comfortable. It may also help to wait until you're fully turned-on before putting anything in your vagina.

For people with a penis, penis-in-vagina sex isn't usually painful. Sometimes friction during sex causes irritation on your penis, but using lube can fix this. If you have pain in your penis or genitals during sex, it could be a sign that something's wrong. Go to a nurse, doctor, or your local Planned Parenthood health center to get checked out. what you should know

There are probably lots of things going through your mind if you are thinking about having sex for the first time. You may be wondering if your body will change or whether it will hurt. Read on to find answers to some of the questions you may have about first-time sex.

## What happens to your body when you have sex?

Your body will not display any telltale signs after you have sex for the first time. The only way anyone will know you've had sex is if you or somebody else tells them.

While having sex, you might breathe heavily and sweat, and your skin could become flushed. These changes are caused by the physical nature of sex. During sex, your vulva may also become swollen due to increased blood flow. After sex, your body will go back to normal, just like it would after exercise.

Most women are born with a hymen, which is a membrane in the vagina that can stretch or tear during exercise, first-time sex, or other activities. During your first time having sex, your hymen might stretch, and you may experience some bleeding if it ruptures. However, bleeding doesn't always occur during first-time sex. Many people have already inadvertently broken their hymen before they ever have sex. If you're worried about bleeding, lying down on a dark-colored towel or cloth can prevent stains.

## There may be some semen that leaks post-sex.

Another reason to urinate after sex.

If you're not using condoms or another form of birth control, you may notice some semen leaking out of the vagina after having sex. Don't worry, it's totally normal.

There's no place else for it to go since your body isn't going to absorb it. To reduce it, you can urinate to expel much of the leakage, Yvonne S. Thornton, M.D., vice chairperson of the department of OB-GYN at Jamaica Hospital Medical Center in New York City told Cosmopolitan. You can also thoroughly wash the area after intercourse to clear it all up.

Your face may look flushed:It's not uncommon to see measle-like pink patches on the face, top of the chest, or occasionally over the whole body post-orgasm, according to Dr. Robert Huizenga, a celebrity physician and author of "Sex, Lies, and STDs."

It's caused by the temporarily increased blood flow in the skin, and usually disappears within minutes — though sometimes it can linger for a full hour after an orgasm, Dr. Huizenga explained.

Cramps can be caused by an orgasm:

As good as sex can be, it can also bring pain, according to a British study. Some people who get their period experience

menstrual-like cramps after intercourse and there are  few common causes.
For some, orgasms actually can cause cramps in the lower abdominal area. Another cause could be due to having a tilted uterus, making it easier for your partner to hit your cervix, causing painCramps after sex are often normal if the pain is mild, but if it's persistent or severe, you'll want to see your gynecologist.

## You can suddenly be very sleepy:

If you find that you need to take a catnap after sex, you're not alone. There are actually several reasons why people feel tired after intimacy.
"One possibility is that you could just be physically exhausted, giving you a similar feeling of fatigue after doing some intense cardio. It's also possible that you're reacting to the change in chemicals that are released during and after an orgasm. The neurochemicals that are released building up to and during an orgasm amp up arousal and excitement, he explained. "Afterward, the profile of chemicals released changes abruptly. Men, more so than women, tend to get very sleepy likely because they respond more to the morphine-like sedating properties of the endorphins,

## It can feel a little itchy down there:

Feeling itchy down there after sex is usually nothing to worry about.
You may feel irritation in that area due to all of the friction that was happening during intercourse. Pubic hair can cause a kind of rug burn when rubbing against another body, bringing

about skin irritation and rashes. If the itchiness or redness doesn't subside, you'll want to schedule an appointment with your doctor.West Palm Beach, Florida, and Charlotte, North CarolinaIt's also possible that you have a sensitivity or allergy to the lube you use or with latex condoms, Maureen Whelihan, M.D., an OB-GYNat the Center for Sexual Health and Education in West Palm Beach, Florida, and Charlotte, North Carolina told Glamour. You can try switching out your lube or condom variety to see it it makes a differenceIt's also possible that you have a sensitivity or allergy to the lube you use or with latex condoms, Maureen Whelihan, M.D., an OB-GYNat the Center for Sexual Health and Education in West Palm Beach, Florida, and Charlotte, North Carolina told Glamour. You can try switching out your lube or condom variety to see it makes a difference.

## Something smells kind of funky.

When you think about it, it makes sense that things start to smell some down there after sex. According to Women's Health magazine, this is because you're combining vaginal secretion of a low pH with semen of a high pH, which produces a chemical reaction with a completely new odor. Plus, the groin is similar to the armpit in that it has a high concentration of sweat glands, meaning that it's likely to get pretty sweaty down there during physical activity. That all adds up to a certain musk. The sex smell is usually not a big deal unless you notice a persistent fishy or foul odor and in that case, you'll want to talk to your gynecologist to make sure you don't have a bacterial imbalance.It’s normal for your vagina to have a slight odor. But if you feel your vagina has a strong odor, such as a fishy smell or an unpleasant smell, it could be a symptom of another health issue or problem.

[1] The odor may be accompanied by other symptoms like itching, burning, irritation, or vaginal discharge.

[2] In general, if you have vaginal odor without other symptoms, the odor may not be abnormal.

[3] There are several common infections found in your vagina that could cause an unpleasant odor or smell, and you can try home remedies as well as professional products to get rid of the odor fast.Do not douche. Douching, which is when you force water or a cleaning agent in your vagina, can actually remove the healthy bacteria in your vagina and can push an infection (if one is present) into your uterus, making your condition worse.

[4]You should also avoid feminine sprays, which are another form of douching that can irritate your vagina or lead to an allergic reaction.

Remember that your vagina naturally cleans itself. As long as you practice good vaginal hygiene, you should not have to force clean it or interfere with its natural cleaning process . Rinse your vagina during your shower or bath. Be sure to keep your vaginal area clean by using water and mild, unscented soap, like Cetaphil, to rinse your vagina, including your labia.

[5]Avoid using harsh soaps on your vagina, with scents, as they can irritate the delicate skin in this area.Wear loose clothing and cotton underwear. This will increase airflow to your groin, especially when you are working out or sweating and prevent moisture buildup, which can then reduce any odors due to sweating or bacteria.

[6]You should also change out of your workout clothing as soon as you are finished with your workout. Do not keep wet, sweaty clothes on any longer than necessary, as this can lead to unpleasant odors.
Always wear clean underwear every day to prevent bacterial growth and odorChange your tampon or pad every four to six hours. Practice good period hygiene by being diligent about changing your tampon or pad every four to six hours. This will prevent a buildup of odor and ensure your vagina does not get irritated during your menstrual cycle.
[8]Changing your tampon frequently will also ensure you do not forget to remove your tampon, which can cause an unpleasant odor and possibly serious health issues.Eat yogurt to promote the growth of yeast. Yogurt contains naturally formed probiotics that can help balance your bacterial secretions in your vagina and in the rest of your body. If you have recurring yeast infections, eating yogurt every day is good, healthy option for eliminating vaginal odor caused by yeast infections.
[9]Check that the yogurt contains live and active cultures to ensure it will help your body produce more yeast.Avoid eating odor causing foods. Eating certain foods and drinks can actually change your vaginal smell, as the foods you consume can cause your body to release certain odors. If you are concerned about your vaginal odor, avoid drinking coffee and alcohol. You should also avoid onions, food made with strong spices, red meat, or dairy.
[10]Keep in mind you would need to consume a high amount of these foods to change your vaginal secretions enough to cause a strong odor. You can try to eliminate these foods and

drinks from your diet to see if you notice a reduction in the odor.

Chapter 2

# bleeding while having sex for the first time

## Will it hurt?

Much of the anxiety surrounding having sex for the first time is centered on whether it will hurt. If you relax, feel comfortable, and pay attention to your body, there probably won't be any pain. What you might feel is a bit of discomfort because this experience is new to you.

If you do feel pain, it is more than likely caused by friction. Friction during penetrative sex occurs when there isn't enough vaginal lubrication to ease the entry of something entering your vagina. Engaging in plenty of foreplay can stimulate the vagina to become more lubricated.

Using lubricant can make intercourse more comfortable and enjoyable.Some girls bleed the first time they have sex, but not all girls do. The reason some girls bleed the first time they have sex is because their hymen stretches or tears. The hymen is a very thin piece of skin-like tissue that partly covers the opening of the vagina. Some girls are born without much of a hymen. Other girls' hymens cover a large portion of the vagina's opening. It all depends on the girl.

Whether a girl bleeds also partly depends on whether the hymen is stretched or torn before sex. It is possible for this to happen from vigorous physical activity, tampon insertion, and masturbation or fingering.

Remember to always use a condom every time you have sex, including the first time, to help protect against pregnancy and STDsThe friction and abrasion of intercourse can easily cause small tears and cuts in sensitive genital tissues.

Childbirth can also cause vaginal tissues to stretch and tear, sometimes making them more vulnerable to injury.

On the first occurrence of sexual intercourse, a small flap of vaginal skin called the hymen is often stretched and broken. The minor bleeding this causes can last 1 to 2 days.

*Chapter 3*

# Vaginal dryness

Dryness is among the most common causes of postcoital bleeding. When the skin is dry it becomes extremely vulnerable to damage. Mucus-producing tissues, such as those in the vagina, are especially vulnerable.

Vaginal dryness is a painful symptom that affects a person's quality of life. It can cause pain during sitting, exercising, peeing and sexual intercourse. Normally, your vaginal lining is lubricated with fluid that helps keep it thick and elastic. Vaginal dryness happens when the tissues in your vagina are dry, thin and not well-moisturized. This leads to discomfort, especially during sex.

Vaginal dryness occurs at any age. It's most common in women or people assigned female at birth (AFAB) during or after menopause when estrogen levels decline. The hormone estrogen helps keep your vaginal lining moisturized and healthy. Low levels of estrogen cause your vaginal walls to become thin and dry. This is a common condition of menopause called vaginal atrophy.

Many safe and effective treatments are available for vaginal dryness.

## What are the possible causes of vaginal dryness?

In many cases, vaginal dryness happens when estrogen levels decrease. This occurs naturally as you age or during menopause. Menopause is when your menstrual period ends and you can no longer become pregnant. When estrogen levels decline, the skin and tissues of your vulva and vagina become thinner and less elastic, and your vagina can become dry.

Certain health conditions or treatments for health conditions can also cause vaginal dryness.

## Vaginal dryness can result from:

- Breastfeeding (chestfeeding) and childbirth.
- Birth control pills or any form of hormonal birth control.
- Cancer treatments including chemotherapy and hormone therapy.
- Diabetes.
- Medications, including anti-estrogen medications (treating uterine fibroids or endometriosis), certain antidepressants and antihistamines (treatment for itchy eyes and runny noses).
- Removal of your ovaries (oophorectomy).
- Sjogren's syndrome (an autoimmune disorder that can cause dryness throughout your body).
- Not being sexually aroused.
- Using scented or perfumed soaps, sprays and washes around or in your vagina.Vaginal dryness is a painful symptom that affects a person's quality of life. It can cause pain during sitting, exercising, peeing and sexual intercourse. Normally, your vaginal lining is lubricated with fluid that helps keep it thick and elastic.What are the possible causes of vaginal dryness?

In many cases, vaginal dryness happens when estrogen levels decrease. This occurs naturally as you age or during menopause. Menopause is when your menstrual period ends and you can no longer become pregnant. When estrogen levels decline, the skin and tissues of your vulva and vagina become thinner and less elastic, and your vagina can become dry.

Why is my vagina dry during sex?

Vaginal dryness is usually most apparent during sexual penetration. Without enough vaginal lubrication, the friction (or rubbing) during sexual intercourse can cause pain and discomfort. Take time before sex to make sure you're fully aroused. Engage in foreplay with your partner and try to relax. Using water-based sexual lubricants can also help.

Unfortunately, painful sex can lead to loss of interest in sex or loss of intimacy with your partner. As embarrassing as it may feel, discuss your symptoms with your partner so they can help you.

## What does a dry vagina feel like?

Vaginal dryness causes discomfort and pain in your vagina, especially during sex. A dry vagina may also cause:

Burning and itching.

Bleeding after sex due to your vaginal wall tissues breaking open.

Soreness in your vulva.

Recurrent urinary tract infections (UTIs) or yeast infections.

Needing to pee more often.

Not wanting to have sex.

Less moisture in your vagina leads to less moisture in your vulvar area (external genitals). This means you can feel dryness or irritation when putting on your underwear or during normal activities like walking or sitting.

How is vaginal dryness diagnosed?

Healthcare providers diagnose vaginal dryness based on your medical history and a physical exam. To find the cause, your provider will ask about your symptoms and any medications you take. They may perform the following tests:

Pelvic exam to view the inside of your vagina, which may be thin, dry and red.

Blood test to determine if hormone levels or a health condition are causing vaginal dryness.

Your provider may also test a sample of your vaginal discharge to rule out other causes or to check for signs of infection.

## How is vaginal dryness treated?

There are many treatments available for vaginal dryness and painful intercourse (dyspareunia) associated with vaginal dryness.

Medications for vaginal dryness

Medications work by either replacing or acting like estrogen in your body. They're available with a prescription only.

Low-dose estrogen cream, ring or tablet: These medications work by replacing estrogen in your body. Creams and tablets are applied directly into your vagina using an applicator. Most are prescribed for daily use until you find relief, then used weekly as needed. Estrogen-containing rings are placed into your vagina for up to three months, then replaced.

Ospemifene (Osphena): This medication is called a selective estrogen modulator (SERM) and is taken by mouth. It acts like estrogen in your body and helps treat painful sex associated with vaginal atrophy.

Dehydroepiandrosterone (DHEA): This is another medication that acts like estrogen in your body. It's a vaginal suppository that helps with painful sex in menopausal people.

Talk to your healthcare provider about the risks and benefits of medication containing estrogen or estrogen-like substances. Estrogen may not be safe for people who've had breast cancer or who are at high risk of breast cancer.

*Chapter 4*

# Will I have an orgasm?

Orgasms give you an extraordinary feeling of pleasure. You orgasm when your sexual desire reaches the state of ejaculation or a discharge that is accumulated by erotic tension. Whether you're a man or a woman, with the right kind of sexual stimulation and intimate touching, an orgasm or a climax is highly possible. However, a lot depends on how you approach this peak of excitement and sensational intensity. Not only is it possible with a physical engagement with your body or your partner, but much of it also relies on your extensive psychological and mental imaginations. Although, an accurate definition or explanation of orgasm still ceases to exist, here's all you need to know about approaching and achieving orgasm.

## What is an Orgasm?

As discussed, an orgasm is a feeling of immense pleasure and a climax of sexual tension and excitement. It is not only caused due to intense sexual stimulation but can also be achieved during any kind of sexual activity, ranging from an act of foreplay to sexual intercourse. Scientifically speaking, orgasms are involuntary actions controlled by the nervous system, where a man or a woman experiences muscular spasms in multiple areas of the body. Once achieved, the person is Borne to have a relaxing experience due to the release of neurohormones oxytocin and prolactin as well as endorphins.

# Types of Orgasms

While the feeling of an orgasm is common to all, the types can differ from one another. Here are some of the most common types of orgasms .

Clitoral: A clitoris is a small part of the female body that is positioned at the top of the vulva. It is a highly sensitive area, which gets wet when rubbed or touched profusely. With an application of highly intensified and fast pressure in a repetitive motion, the orgasm begins to intensify in both the male and the female.

Anal: Anal Orgasms are more frequent in men because of the prostate, but can be achieved by anyone with a simple rub or stimulation around the openings of the anus.

Vaginal: Vaginal orgasm is one of the best ways for women to orgasm. As you intensify your touch and identify your G-spot, you can apply direct stimulation with the help of a partner or engage in self-stimulation to lead to a state of climax.Combo: A Combo orgasm is a blend of both clitoral and vaginal stimulation. This is the easiest way to reach an orgasm for women but sometimes men also enjoy it in the process.

Erogenous Zones: The erogenous zones can only be found through experimentation. Parts of the body such as the neck, teeth on your nipples, when touched, help in intensifying the pleasure and sometimes even help achieve an orgasm. All one needs to do is kiss the neck or touch the sensitive areas on the body.According to an American sex researcher Better Dodson, there are also forms of orgasms that can be commonly achieved by both men and women through just genital stimulation.

That being said, here are 5 other kinds of orgasms.

Pressure Orgasms: Pressure orgasms are the kind that is independent of a partner. It is achieved through an indirect stimulation that is initiated with applied pressure.

Combination Orgasms: Combination Orgasms are a blend of different orgasms experienced at the same time and cannot be identified specifically.

Multiple Orgasms: Multiple Orgasms are a series of climaxes reached in a short period of time.

Tension Orgasms: Tension Orgasms are felt through direct stimulation and are achieved when the muscles and the body are tensed.

Relaxation Orgasms: Relaxation Orgasms are achieved when the body is calm and free from all the tension during a sexual activity.

Male Orgasms:

How to achieve?

Orgasms in men are induced by a steroid hormone called testosterone, produced in the testicles. While it may seem easy for a man to achieve an orgasm, it is however extremely complex and procedural. Besides the necessity for a sexual desire, there are many other things that are to be accomplished in the process. That being said, here are 4 steps for a man to follow in order to achieve an orgasm.

1.Arousal or Excitement – In this stage, the man jumps right into a state of excitement and sexual arousal, due to a sexual desire. This can be triggered through any form of sexual interest and/or different forms of foreplay. While in a state of arousal, the male genital i.e. the penis, is bound to harden as the blood rush from the arteries to the penis is faster than the usual flow and the veins in the penis that normally drain blood out disable the outflow of the blood from the penis.

2.Plateau – After continuous stimulation, the male body prepares itself for an ejaculation, which can go on from 30 seconds to 2 minutes. Just seconds before the orgasm, the male urethra will release a clear fluid. This pre-ejaculatory fluid changes the pH level of the Urethra that improves the quality of the sperm.
3.Orgasm – While the male body reaches its climax at this stage, the orgasm is divided into two parts i.e. Emission and ejaculation. Emission is the point where there is no looking back for the man. At this stage, the male body must move forward to the stage of ejaculation.
4. Resolution – At this stage, the body is relaxed and the accumulated tension will fade. Slowly and steadily the penis will lose its erection. This is followed by a refractory period, during which the male body cannot achieve another erection. However, when it comes to women, they can achieve multiple orgasms one after the other.
Female Orgasms: How to achieve?
When it comes to female orgasms, there's a whole lot of patience and understanding that goes with the necessary sexual stimulation and intensity. Unlike men, women don't always reach an orgasm in the process of sexual intercourse. That said, it becomes extremely important to understand the female climax, in order to achieve the ultimate sense of pleasure. Here are the 4 stages involved in female orgasms.
1. Excitement – At this stage of arousal, blood flow is higher in the genital and sexually sensitive areas in a female body. With the increase in heart rate, blood pressure and breathing, the women feel a sense of excitement and a gush of pleasure.
2. Plateau – Plateau is the stage where women arousal rate builds and reaches the peak of its sexual tension. The sexual

stimulation that arouses the woman takes over all other senses in the body.

3. Orgasm – Finally when the female body cannot hold it anymore, it releases all the sexual tension accumulated due to continuous sexual intercourse or self-stimulation. A deep sense of warmth and pleasure is released from the pelvic area that spreads to the entire body.

4. Resolution – Finally, the body of the woman is relaxed and the blood is released to other parts of the body, making the genitals free of all the tension. Everything from the heart rate to blood pressure to breathing decreases. However, a female can engage in another set of orgasm, almost immediately.Well, reaching a state of orgasm is simply an understanding between our bodily senses and our sexual desires. Once the two are on the same tangent, nothing can really slow down or hinder the process.

When you and your partner are figuring out how to have sex for the first time, you might believe that it will be as magical as it is often depicted in the movies. However, it's possible that your first time won't be nearly as smooth or well choreographed.

For many people, their first time is an awkward and somewhat uncomfortable affair. On top of that, both of you might be nervous. Under circumstances like these, it can be difficult to achieve an orgasm. This is perfectly normal. In fact, sex without orgasm can be quite enjoyable and might be a good way for you and your partner to connect further.

*Chapter 5*

# Can I get pregnant having sex for the first time?

Tons of people wonder whether you can get pregnant at first time sex or not? The answer to this million-dollar question is YES! it is totally true! Yes, you read it right, first time sex can cause pregnancy. Any young lady who has unprotected vaginal intercourse risks getting to be pregnant, regardless of whether it's her first time engaging in sexual relations or the 100th time. It's even conceivable to wind up pregnant before regularly having a period.Pregnancy can happen when discharge or pre-discharge gets in the vagina or on the vulva. And, this can happen at any or all times you have an intercourse. Therefore, if both the partners are fertile and as this happens first time sex can cause pregnancy for sure!
The passage of semen otherwise called sperm or discharge inside the vagina is the reason for pregnancy. The utilization of conception prevention and condoms each time while engaging in sexual relations can help you in maintaining a strategic distance from pregnancy. With such huge numbers of bits of gossip circling around sex, it is relatively incomprehensible for a man to observe reality from the false. The ideal method for guaranteeing that you are having safe sex is to get your certainties straight. It is a result of the absence of information that young ladies don't know whether first time sex can cause pregnancy or notMany people around the world think that first time sex can cause pregnancy. This is

a long way from reality. Pregnancy relies upon the fertility of both men and women. It may take months or even a long time of frantic striving for a few ladies to consider while others may imagine at whatever point they engage in sexual relations regardless of whether it is their first time and they have no want of getting pregnant either. However as engaging in sexual relations without the utilization of contraception can get a young lady pregnant regardless of whether she is having intercourse out of the blue or has had it a lot of times previously.

Remember: Pregnancy is plausible each time a lady and a man participates in intercourse. The main prerequisite is that a sperm achieves an egg. Indeed, even young ladies who haven't discharged may wind up fruitful on the off chance that they have discharged an egg out of the blue, making it feasible for them to get pregnant at first sex.

Chapter 6

# Risks Involved

Other than the worry of can first time sex cause pregnancy or not, sexual activities also predisposes you get STIs or sexually transmitted contaminations each time you have unprotected sex. Both STIs and pregnancy can stay away by amending utilization of condoms each time while engaging in sexual functioning.

Prevention:

Condoms are the most secure method for warding off the two STDs and pregnancy in the event that you expect on engaging in sexual relations. Regardless of whether you are utilizing an elective type of anti-conception medication, it is best to tell your accomplice ahead of time that condoms are not discretionary and are in actuality vital. Therefore, make sure you learn how to use condoms for male & female.You can likewise bring down your danger of pregnancy by utilizing crisis preventative pills which are additionally known by the name of a day after pills or next day contraceptives.

What are the signs of pregnancy?

The most, clear indication of pregnancy is feeling the loss of a period after you have had unprotected sex. It is best to take a pregnancy test on the off chance that you have a late period.

Here's all you have to know about whether first time sex can cause pregnancy

What sort of sex can cause pregnancy?

First time sex can cause pregnancy – the likelihood increases if you take part in a specific sort of sexual activity. For example, having vaginal sex wherein the semen enters the vagina or any intercourse actions and activities that comes full circle in the semen being discharged into the vagina.

However, taking an interest in other sexual exercises like kissing is not liable to get a young lady pregnant whether it is her first time or not.

There's a myth in some societies that you can't get pregnant when you have sex for the first time. This is false. If you have already started getting your period, you can get pregnant if you have sex.

If you don't want to become pregnant, you should use a birth control method whenever you engage in sexual intercourse.

*Chapter 7*

# Contraception for having sex for the first time

contraception is a way to prevent pregnancy after unprotected sex. Often called the morning-after pill, emergency contraceptive pills (ECPs) are pills that can be taken up to 120 hours (5 days) after having unprotected sex. Some types of emergency contraception work best when taken within 72 hours (3 days) after intercourse.

First-time sex: ways to reduce anxiety

If you're having sex for the first time, you may feel anxious. This is common and completely normal. There are lots of things you can do to deal with this anxiety.

Right partner

Some studies show that you are more likely to have both psychological and physical satisfaction when you have sex with someone you trust and with whom you have a steady relationship. Being with someone you trust can help you feel safer and more in control of the situation.

## Cozy place

One thing is for certain — with so many different positions, devices you both can add, and places to have sex, your sex life should be far from boring. Get creative! Be spontaneous and have some fun getting the excitement back.

Note: Some of these might be better to fantasize about than to do! No matter what you do, remember to be safe and take all necessary precautions. Sex can be steamy without being needlessly risky.

- On top of the kitchen table.
- On top of the washing machine.
- In the file room at work—there is just something about the thrill of getting caught.
- In your unfinished home.
- Or in someone else's unfinished home — sneaking into a house that is still under construction in the middle of the night sounds even better.
- At the laundromat.
- In an open field during a heavy fog.
- In your office (with the door locked of course) (or not, depending on what you like.)

If you want to have sex but feel anxious about it, plan to do it in a place you find comfortable. An unfamiliar or uncomfortable location could make it hard to focus on what's going on and enjoy what's happening.

*Chapter 8*

# Foreplay

Anxiety about the first time you have sex is pretty common. However, foreplay may help reduce your anxious feelings. Foreplay involves a lot of kissing and touching, which can help you feel more comfortable with your own body as well as your partner's. First and foremost, your go-to foreplay routine shouldn't start in the bedroom. It can start with slow, intimate kissing and touching each other in your living room making your way to full-fledged sex on the bed.Sexting can be a hot form of foreplay, especially when it includes teasing your partner on the other side of the screen. Let your partner know what you are going to do to them or what you want them to do to you. Let them imagine little scenes in their head and they will be all too excited to get home for the final showdown because they're already so turned on with all the sexting.Dirty talk is hot! But a photograph can leave a lot less to the imagination. Say your partner loves it when you send them a sexy picture of yourself. Why not do exactly that when you're in the mood? Set the mood by sending them a sexy picture of you or what you'd wear in the night and let the rest do the talking.Wear your favourite lingerie

This will come in handy if you are planning on using the previous tip. Even if you have no intention of sending your partner a sexy selfie, sexy lingerie will any day put you in the mood and increase your own anticipation for what could come later that night. Take a shower together

While your partner's in the shower, feel free to hop in! Shower sex doesn't have to be the end goal of this either. Having fun in the water and getting excited for whatever's to happen outside of the shower is exciting all in itself. However, we're not against trying to make shower sex work — just don't hurt yourself! If you don't already turn up your speakers while you're having sex, now might be the time to start. Whatever kind of music turns you both on, whether it's R&B, country, slow songs, or even show tunes (hey, Brittany in Glee singing Britney is beyond sexy), turn it up and use the music as the rhythm of all of your moves. Dance around the kitchen and sing along. Having fun together is sexy! Making a playlist together of your favorite songs to get down to can also be a form of foreplay on its own.

# Chapter 9

## Take it slow

A lot of anxiety can come from trying to rush sex to get to the next step. You might find yourself thinking about what you should be doing and what you should do next. If so, take a moment to center yourself and focus on the present, letting things happen naturally.

To get your guy to last longer, have him start slow, Men's Fitness magazine suggests. Tell him to aim for one thrust every few seconds, then gradually (like, every two minutes) take it up a notch, to the point where there's a thrust every second or so. If he feels like he's going to come, he should stop thrusting and wait a few seconds until he can control himself and start up again.A round of vigorous foreplay before sex can work wonders, according to Cosmopolitan magazine. Not only can you orgasm, which might make you more likely to come again during sex, but getting him to ejaculate before the main event should delay the finish line. For many guys, it takes a certain amount of time to "recharge," which means you should have plenty of time to be satisfied.

Some people are in a hurry to achieve orgasm. Taking your time and enjoying the journey can make sex a more relaxed and enjoyable experience.As much as aggressive sex can be fun, it's not all the time that adrenaline is pumping for that kind of sex. Sex is a multi-sensory experience, and when you slow it down, you can enjoy it more…the sights, sounds, smells, tastes and touches.

That is part of the benefits of slow sex that kind of sex with slow music playing in the background.

Slow sex can bring your lovemaking experience to new heights. Of course, this is not to say that you can't feel things with fast sex, it's just that you feel it more with slow sex.

Here are some reasons why slow sex can quickly become a favourite:

As much as aggressive sex can be fun, it's not all the time that adrenaline is pumping for that kind of sex. Sex is a multi-sensory experience, and when you slow it down, you can enjoy it more…the sights, sounds, smells, tastes and touches.

You can feel and savour every touch: Slow, erotic touching can ignite a passion and hunger in the body like no other…research has shown.

The sex lasts longer: Slow sex unfolds because there's no rush. It becomes an adventure and allows for more exploration of each other's bodies. Many times the focus of sex is penetration. Slower sex allows you to focus on so many other avenues of pleasure.

Eye contact: Slow sex enables the opportunity for sustained eye contact and this turns up the intensity of emotions and sensations.

Potential for orgasm: Since most women take a longer time to orgasm than men, taking your time during sex increases the likelihood that both of you will have time to reach orgasm, maybe even simultaneously…. It is important to keep clitoral stimulation in mind hereCan slow down orgasm: Slow sex can be especially helpful if you're concerned about early ejaculation or erectile dysfunction because there is no "race to the finish line". Slowing down helps you to remain aware of your own arousal.

Creates room for creativity: Slow sex creates room for more authenticity and creativity. You can introduce different sexual accessories or toys. The options to play together are endless and slowing down ensures you will have more time to think outside the box.

Try again later

It's very common to have a less-than-perfect first time. However, that doesn't mean that sex will always be bad. Any number of things can contribute to an experience that doesn't quite live up to your expectations.

You can always try again later when you are feeling more comfortable. However, you're under no obligation to commit to a next time, either. The best time to have sex is when you're sure you want it, not just when your partner wants you to.

## Chapter 10

# Avoiding STIs

The risk of contracting infections is much higher if you don't use protection when you have sex. Some sexually transmitted infections (STIs) include:

Chlamydia
HIV/AIDS
Hepatitis B and C
Genital herpes
Syphilis
Gonorrhea

While some of these diseases can be treated with antibiotic medication, some are incurable and can have serious health implications. HIV has no cure, but there are medications that can suppress the virus almost completely. Left untreated, HIV can develop into AIDS, which has no cure. Using condoms when you engage in sexual intercourse will greatly reduce the risk of contracting an STI.

Contraception

Unless you're planning to have a baby, you should use contraceptive methods to reduce the likelihood of pregnancy. You can opt for barrier methods such as condoms, diaphragms, or caps. These stop sperm from reaching the egg. Other methods, like the birth control pill, alter your hormones to ensure that an egg is not released. Only condoms protect against both pregnancy and STIs, but it's important to remember that no protection method is 100 percent effective.

If you're puzzled by how to have sex for the first time, that's a totally normal way to feel. It's common to be anxious, but being with the right partner in a cozy place and taking things slowly can help. Be sure to practice safe sex to avoid unplanned pregnancies and sexually transmitted infections.

# Conclusion

Sex and sexuality are a part of life. Aside from reproduction, sex can be about intimacy and pleasure. Sexual activity, penile-vaginal intercourse (PVI), or masturbation, can offer many surprising benefits to all facets of your life:
So, how can you be sure that someone is actually sex positive, and how can you communicate that yourself? Well, there are a few things you can do to be a little more confident that you and another person are on the same page.Sexual health is more than avoiding diseases and unplanned pregnancies. It's also about recognizing that sex can be an important part of your life, according to theEveryone's "first time" is different. But one of the most important parts of being prepared for sex is making sure you use birth control and condoms to help prevent pregnancy and STDs. Here's what happens when you lose your virginity.It's a good idea to cut your nails beforehand. Wash your hands properly before you start. Use a new condom for every sexual activity, even if you don't ejaculate. Women should pee before and immediately after sex to reduce the chances of urinary tract infections - cuddling can be postponed by a minute. Men should wait 15 minutes after intercourse to urinate. Clean up any body fluids with a wet towel or tissue once you're done.

www.ingramcontent.com/pod-product-compliance
Lightning Source LLC
LaVergne TN
LVHW020534160826
845677LV00015B/4051
*9798844344930*